Dumby, Dum, Dum

Lisa Meuser

COPYRIGHT © 2021 BY LISA MEUSER

ALL RIGHTS RESERVED

ALL RIGHTS RESERVED. EXCEPT FOR USE IN REVIEW, NO PORTION OF THIS BOOK MAY BE INTRODUCED INTO A RETRIEVAL SYSTEM OR TRANSMITTED IN ANY FORM WITHOUT THE EXPRESS PERMISSION OF THE AUTHOR

ILLUSTRATED BY MYBORDERLESS

PRINTED IN THE UNITED STATES OF AMERICA

This Book Belongs to:

_____

Ellen, the dragon, went dumby, dum, dum all day long. She danced, she blew fire, and she sang songs. She was such a happy little dragon, dumby, dum, dumming, all the day through. She never really knew there were other things to do.

Then along came a bird and squawked, "Why can't you fly, just like me. It's really as easy as one, two, threeeeee."

"I'm too busy to fly. I have things to do. Like sing, and dance and blow fire at youuuu!" Then off Ellen went down the dirt lane and under the birch tree, dumby dum dum, as happy as can be.

Then she thought, "I have such big wings, why CAN'T I fly?" So Ellen began to sigh, sigh, sigh. She wanted to go way up and soar through the sky, with the birds and the bees and the pesky house flies.

She wiggled and waggled, jumped and fell. No matter how hard she flapped, it did not go well. Ellen began to whimper and cry. All the other animals could hear her sigh, sigh, sigh...

The bird flew over and started to squeak, "Flying is as easy as one, two, three. One. Jump up in the air. Two. Wiggle everywhere. Three. Flap your wings; then you're flying with no care...

So Ellen jumped, wiggled and flapped her wings around, but then she fell, dumby, dum, dum, straight to the ground. She huffed, and she puffed with a big hefty sigh, but all the other animals chanted, "Don't give up, give it another try!"

Ellen jumped. She wiggled and flapped her wings, but again she fell dumby, dum, dum to the ground. She took an even more profound sigh, and the animals began to chant even louder. " Try. Try. Try!!!"

"Ellen, don't give up. Try. Try. Try. Just like me." The little Bird sang as she wiggled her wings and flew away, whistling in the wind past the birch tree.

Ellen was more determined than ever. She counted to three. "One. Jump in the air. Two. Wiggle everywhere. Three. Flap your wings; then you're flying with no care."

Then with a little will and a whole lot of desire, she was up, up, up in the air, her heart full of fire. Ellen was flying! Soaring through the sky. After so many tries, she did it, and there were no more sighs.

The animals of the forest cheered with love as Ellen hovered way up above. She flew high. She flew low. She flew fast. She flew slow. She flew everywhere singing her usual song. Dumby, dum, dum all day long... But with a little extra boopity, boo, boo because now she had just soooo much to do!

The End

Manufactured by Amazon.ca
Bolton, ON